AIR MAIL

Samantha Berger

Snail
Mail

pictures by Julia Patton

RP|KIDS
PHILADELPHIA

For PHRAN NOVELLI
who always slows down
to read my books- SB

To FRANKIE + LOLLY
my favourite little
snails- JP

Running Press Kids
Hachette Book Group
1290 Avenue of the Americas, New York, NY 10104
www.runningpress.com/rpkids
@RP_Kids
Printed in China

First Edition: August 2018

Published by Running Press Kids, an imprint of Perseus Books, LLC, a subsidiary of Hachette Book Group, Inc.

The Hachette Speakers Bureau provides a wide range of authors for speaking events.
To find out more, go to www.hachettespeakersbureau.com or call (866) 376-6591.

The publisher is not responsible for websites (or their content) that are not owned by the publisher.

Design by T. L. Bonaddio.
USA Antique Map © GettyImages/nicoolay

Library of Congress Control Number: 2016956221

ISBNs: 978-0-7624-6251-3 (hardcover), 978-0-7624-6252-0 (e-book), 978-0-7624-9161-2 (e-book), 978-0-7624-9162-9 (e-book)

Printer 1010

10 9 8 7 6 5 4 3 2 1

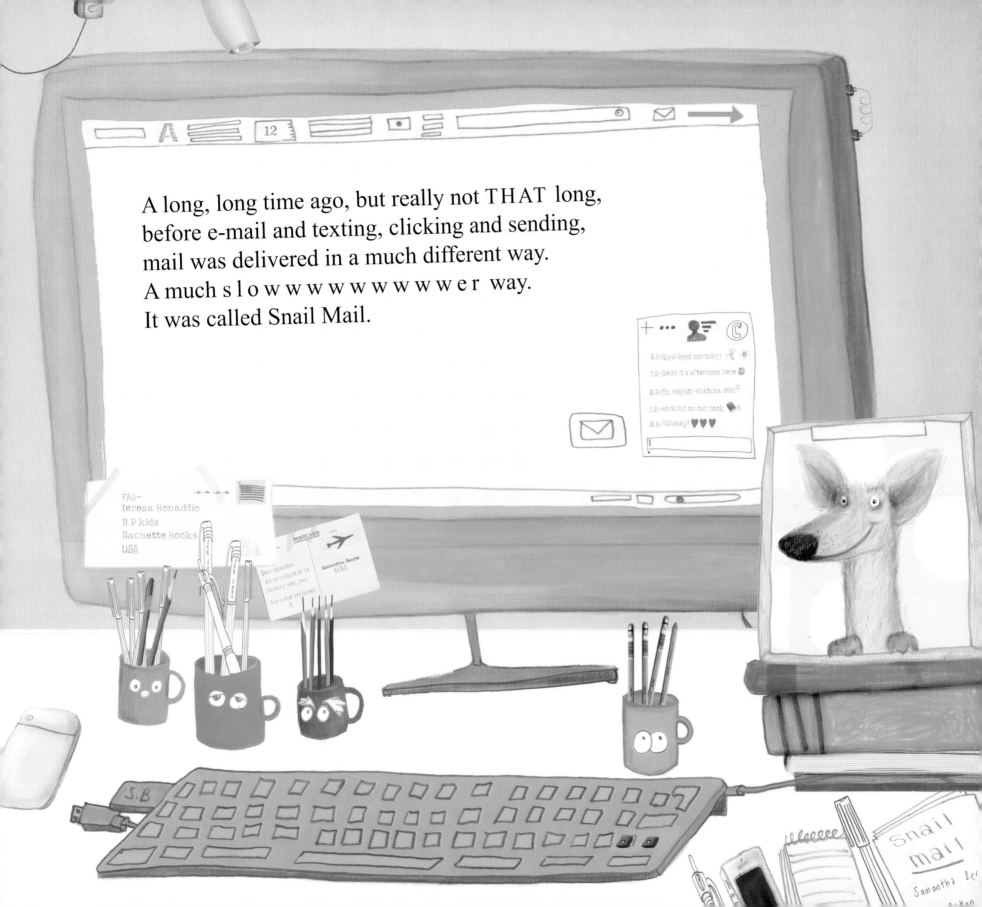

A long, long time ago, but really not THAT long,
before e-mail and texting, clicking and sending,
mail was delivered in a much different way.
A much s l o w w w w w w w w e r way.
It was called Snail Mail.

Many suspected it was called Snail Mail because snails delivered it.

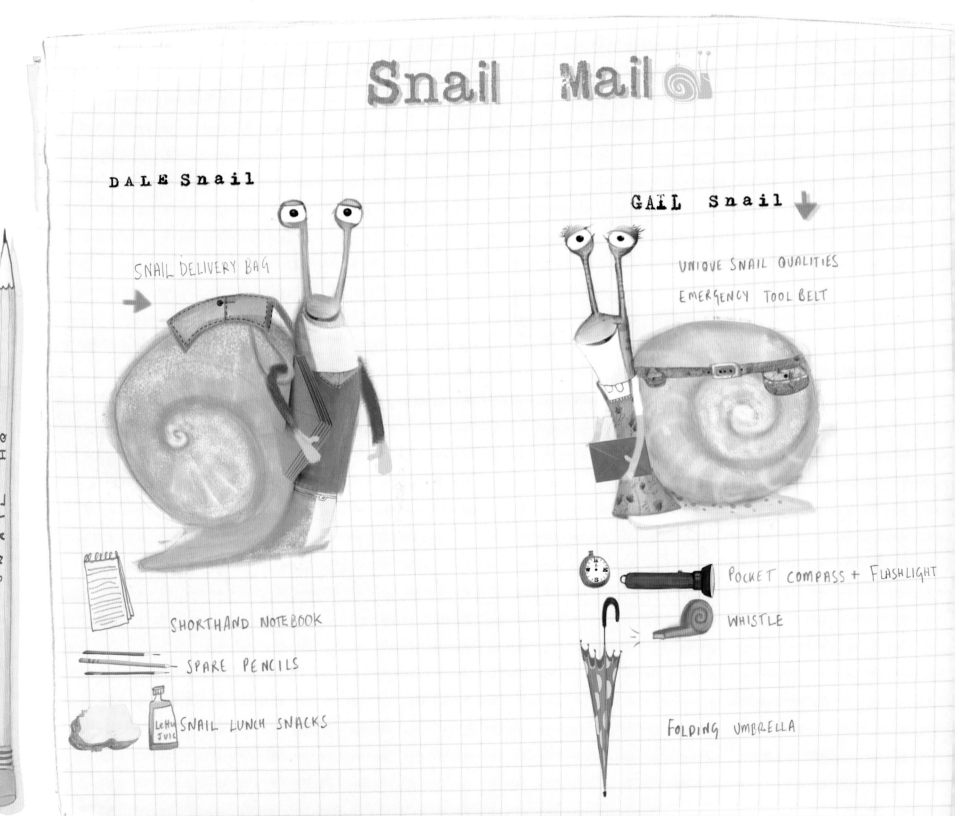

Snail Mail

DALE Snail
SNAIL DELIVERY BAG
SHORTHAND NOTEBOOK
SPARE PENCILS
SNAIL LUNCH SNACKS

GAIL Snail
UNIQUE SNAIL QUALITIES
EMERGENCY TOOL BELT
POCKET COMPASS + FLASHLIGHT
WHISTLE
FOLDING UMBRELLA

Snails like Dale Snail, Gail Snail, Colonel McHale Snail, and Umbérto.

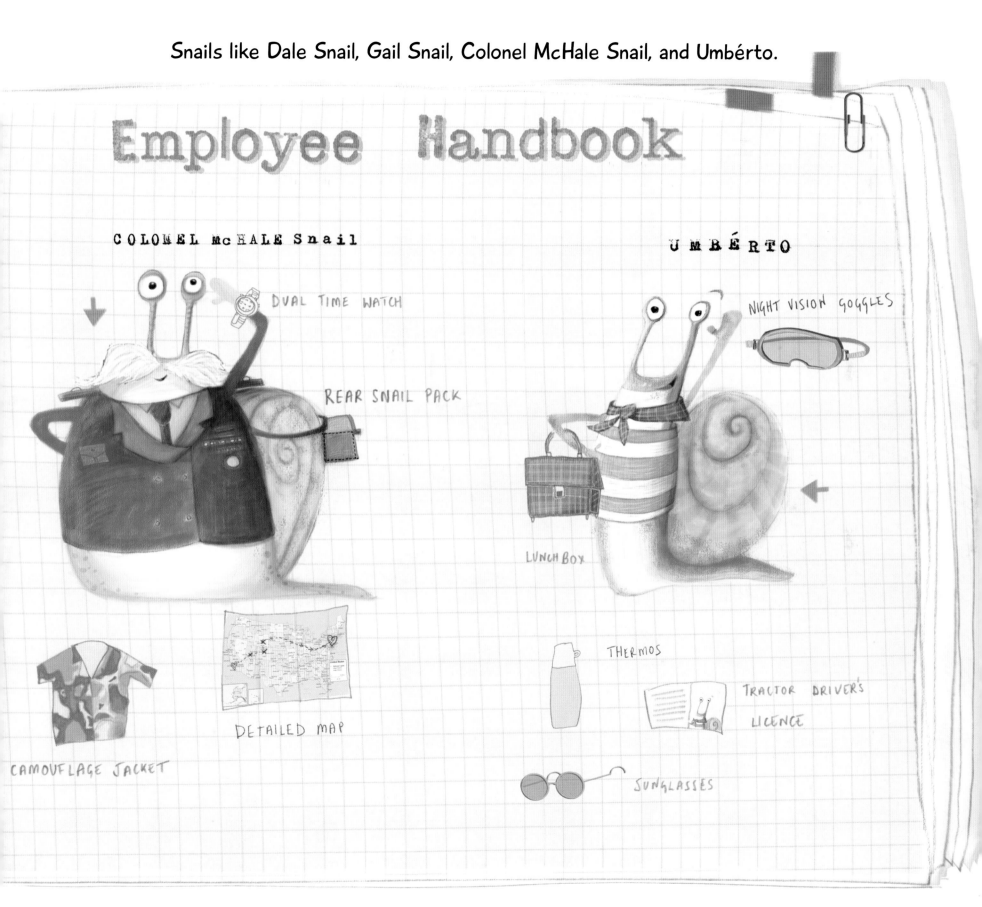

Employee Handbook

COLONEL McHALE Snail

DUAL TIME WATCH

REAR SNAIL PACK

CAMOUFLAGE JACKET

DETAILED MAP

UMBÉRTO

NIGHT VISION GOGGLES

LUNCH BOX

THERMOS

TRACTOR DRIVER'S LICENCE

SUNGLASSES

Although it took much longer, everyone agreed that some things were just A LITTLE more special when they were delivered by Snail Mail.

Things like birthday cards,
notes to Santa,
postcards,
and love letters.

One such letter was made by a Girl who loved a Boy.
It was a card made with her own hands,
written in her own handwriting,
and sealed with her own kiss.
It even smelled a little bit like her.

It HAD to be delivered by Snail Mail.

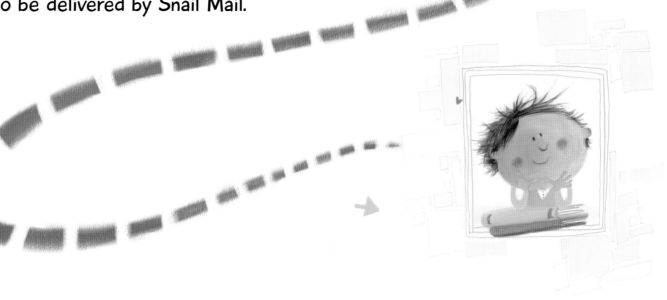

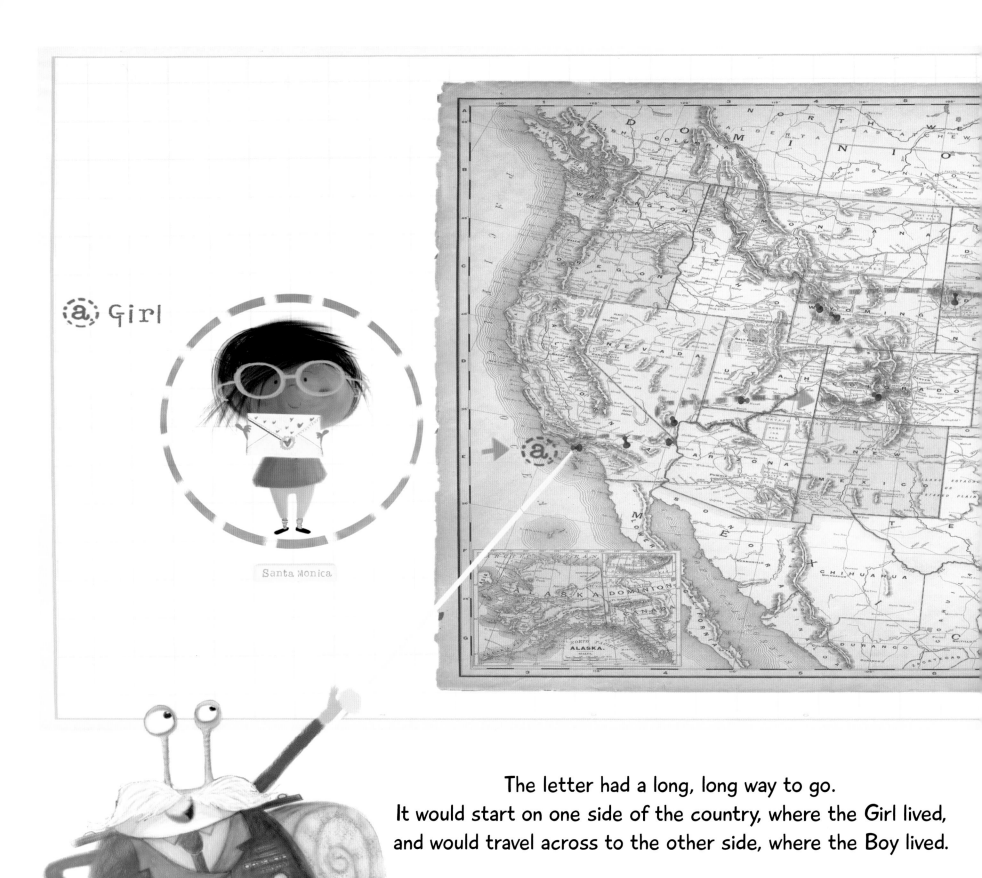

ⓐ Girl

Santa Monica

The letter had a long, long way to go.
It would start on one side of the country, where the Girl lived,
and would travel across to the other side, where the Boy lived.

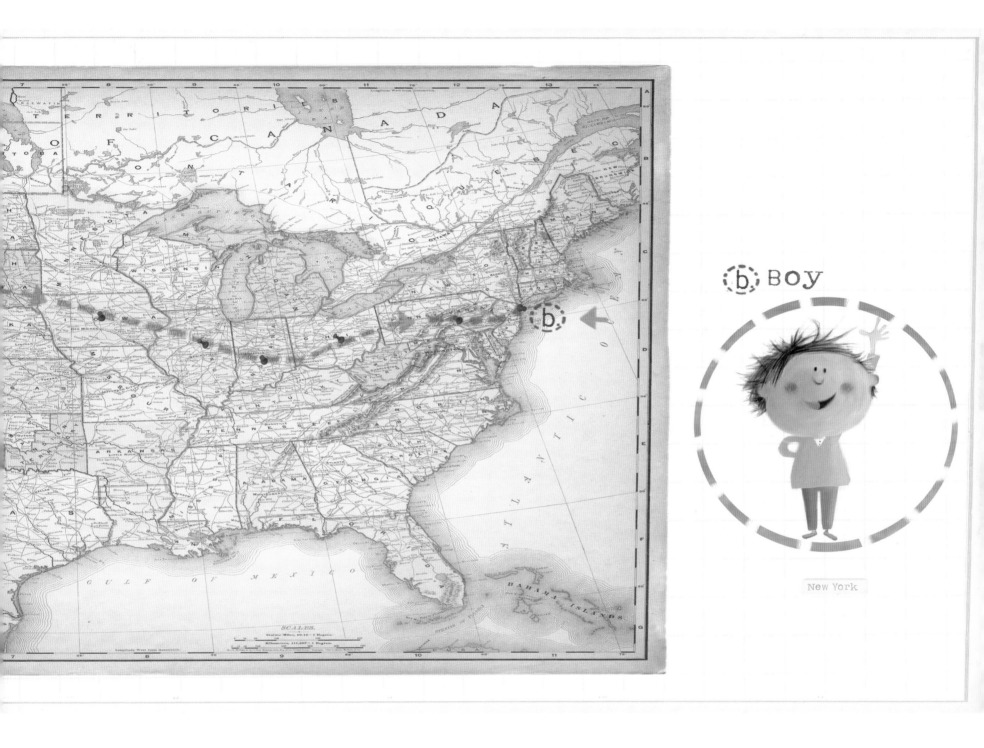

b (b) BOY

New York

It was a very big journey.

ESPECIALLY for a snail.

They knew it would be a challenge.
They knew there were many risks.
But when they saw the Girl's face as she
mailed her letter, they knew they had to try.

Dale Snail looked
determined.

Gail Snail looked
ready.

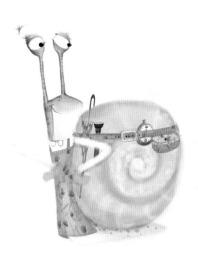

Umbérto looked
like he had been working out.

*wink

"Snails, take your places!" said Colonel McHale Snail.

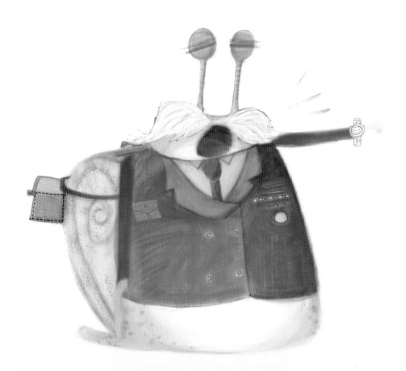

The four snails each slithered underneath a corner
of the envelope and carefully lifted it up.
Barely.

"On your marks. Get set . . . GO!" commanded Colonel McHale Snail.
It was a slow-mo go.
Slowly, slowly, S L O W W W W W L Y,
they inched forward.
"Remember the Snail Mail Promise," said the Colonel.
"Neither rain, nor snow, nor heat, nor hail will stop a snail from bringing the mail."

They started their journey by crossing the desert.
There was bright golden light in the day and a sea of silver stars at night.

There were spiky, prickly plants and giant building-block rocks.
The envelope kept them shaded from the hot sun
and protected them from all kinds of curious creatures.

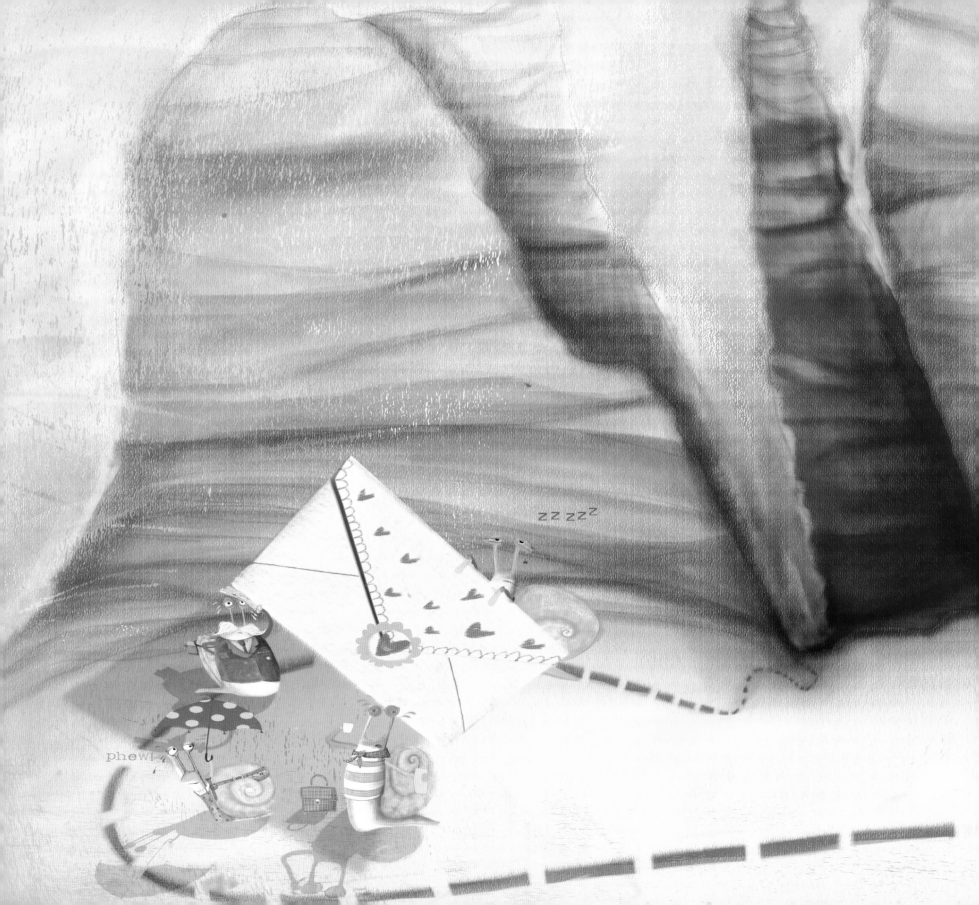

phew!

ZZ ZZ^Z

Steadily, they made their way through red rock canyons,
with dripping sand castles and rippling dunes.
And though they were very tired and very thirsty,
the whole time they chanted their Snail Mail Motto:

"Neither snow, nor rain, nor heat, nor hail
will stop a snail from bringing the mail."

Next, they trekked over vast mountains and through thick pine groves,
past shimmering cool lakes and sweet green meadows.
And every day, they saw a rainbow—
sometimes even a double rainbow.

The sunsets here were so breathtaking, even Colonel McHale had
tears in his eyes, but he insisted it was only allergies.

*sniff

And even though their progress was very slow . . .
there was something special about slowing down . . .
to look around . . .
and notice . . .

Jackson Hole

Mitchell Corn Palace

Slowpoke Lane

what an amazing place the country was.

They wound their way through cornfields and crossed flat flatlands.
They used the envelope to surf on the wind and to catch rides with the sparrows.

Sometimes it poured.

Sometimes it blizzarded.

Sometimes it got blazing hot.

Sometimes it pelted ice.

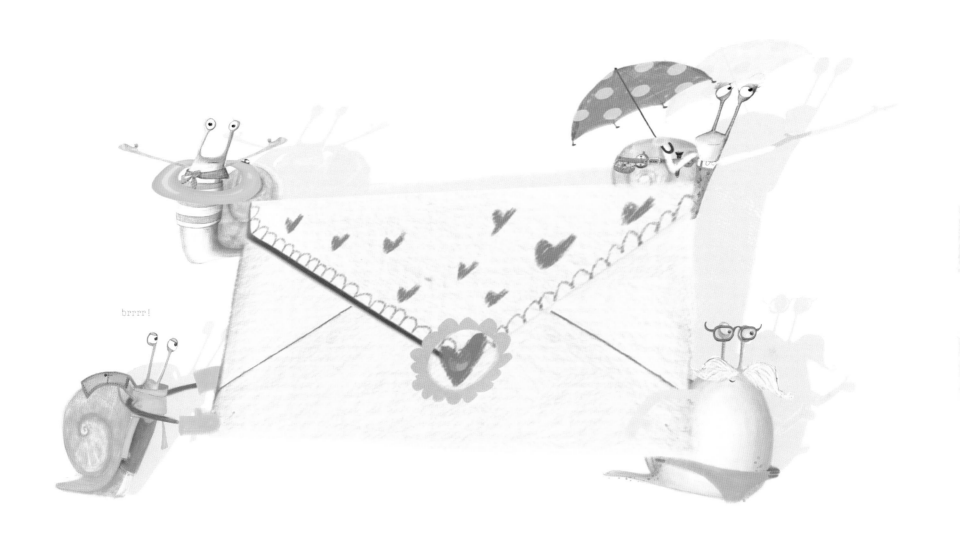

Sometimes it did all of those things in ONE DAY!
But the snails were determined to deliver the mail.

And finally . . .
in a giant city, down a
long narrow street filled
with numbers and letters
and sounds and smells
and honking and beeping,
the Snail Mail found the Boy.

superstore →

eep
eep

GO

WALK →

superstore →

TAXI

→ subway

The Boy opened the envelope
and saw the Girl's letter.

He saw it was made with her own hands,
written in her own handwriting,
and sealed with her own kiss.
It even smelled a little bit like her.
When the snails saw the Boy's face as he opened the letter,
they knew their journey was worth it.

And there was also a letter waiting for THEM.
It was from the United States Snail Mail Office.
It was written in fancy letters and
sealed with a shiny seal.

It even smelled official.

*sniff

Inside, they found a letter congratulating them
and four golden medals for good service.

It was something they could have only gotten through Snail Mail.

Neither snow, nor rain, nor heat, nor hail could stop those snails from bringing the mail.
So they headed home to tell their tale . . .

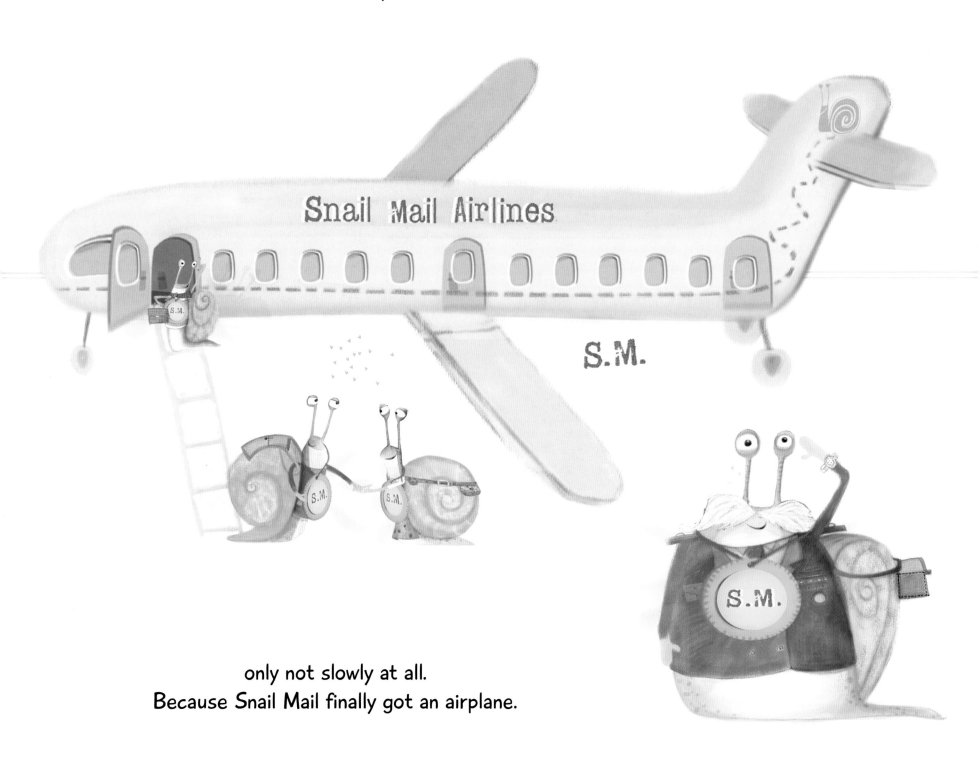

only not slowly at all.
Because Snail Mail finally got an airplane.

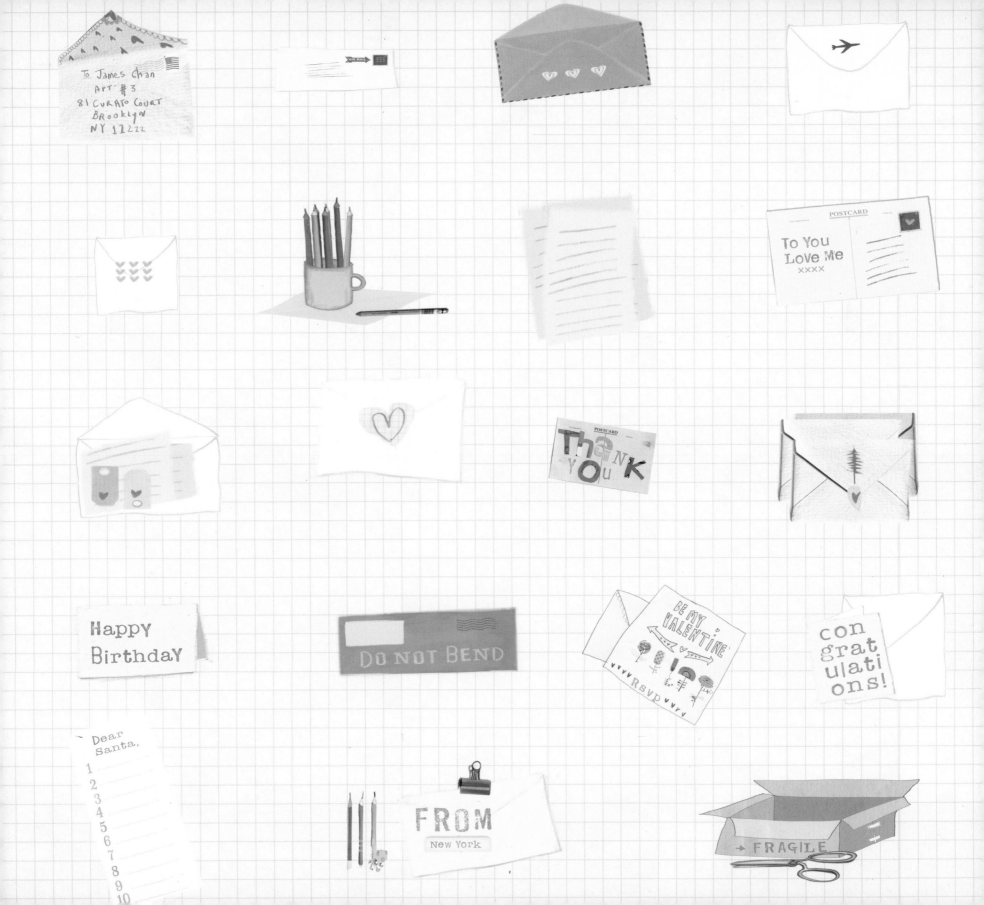